William Cullen Bryant

The Song of the Sower

William Cullen Bryant

The Song of the Sower

ISBN/EAN: 9783744769020

Printed in Europe, USA, Canada, Australia, Japan

Cover: Foto ©Andreas Hilbeck / pixelio.de

More available books at **www.hansebooks.com**

THE

Song of the Sower.

BY

WILLIAM CULLEN BRYANT.

Illustrated with Forty-two Engravings on Wood.

NEW YORK:

D. APPLETON & COMPANY.

MDCCCLXXI

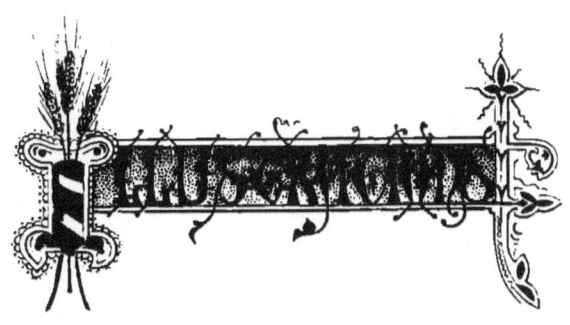

LIST OF ILLUSTRATIONS.

8

THE SONG OF THE SOWER.

I.

THE maples redden in the sun;
In autumn gold the beeches stand;

9

Rest, faithful plough,
    thy work is done
Upon the teeming land.
Bordered with trees whose
    gay leaves fly
On every breath that sweeps
    the sky,
The fresh dark acres fur-
    rowed lie,
And ask the sower's hand.

Loose the tired steer and let
    him go
To pasture where the gentians
    blow,
And we, who till the grateful
    ground,
Fling we the golden shower
    around.

11

II.

Fling wide the generous grain; we fling
O'er the dark mould the green of spring.
For thick the emerald blades shall grow,
When first the March winds melt the snow,
And to the sleeping flowers, below,
  The early bluebirds sing.

Fling wide the grain ; we give the fields
 The ears that nod in summer's gale,
The shining stems that summer gilds,

The harvest that o'erflows the vale,
And swells, an amber sea, between
The full-leaved woods, its shores of green.

Hark! from the murmuring clods I hear
Glad voices of the coming year;
The song of him who binds the grain,
The shout of those that load the wain.

14

And from the distant grange there comes
The clatter of the thresher's flail,

And steadily the
    millstone hums
Down in the
    willowy vale.

III.

Fling wide the golden shower; we trust
The strength of armies to the dust,
This peaceful lea may haply yield
Its harvest for the tented field.

17

Ha! feel ye not your fingers thrill,
  As o'er them, in the yellow grains,
Glide the warm drops of blood that fill,
  For mortal strife, the warrior's veins;

Such as, on Solferino's day,
Slaked the brown sand and flowed away;—
Flowed till the herds, on Mincio's brink,
Snuffed the red stream and feared to drink;—
Blood that in deeper pools shall lie,
    On the sad earth, as time grows gray,
When men by deadlier arts shall die,
And deeper darkness blot the sky
        Above the thundering fray;

And realms, that hear the battle-cry,
　　Shall sicken with dismay ;
And chieftains to the war shall lead
Whole nations, with the tempest's speed,
　　To perish in a day :—

Till man, by love and mercy taught,
Shall rue the wreck his fury wrought,
And lay the sword away.

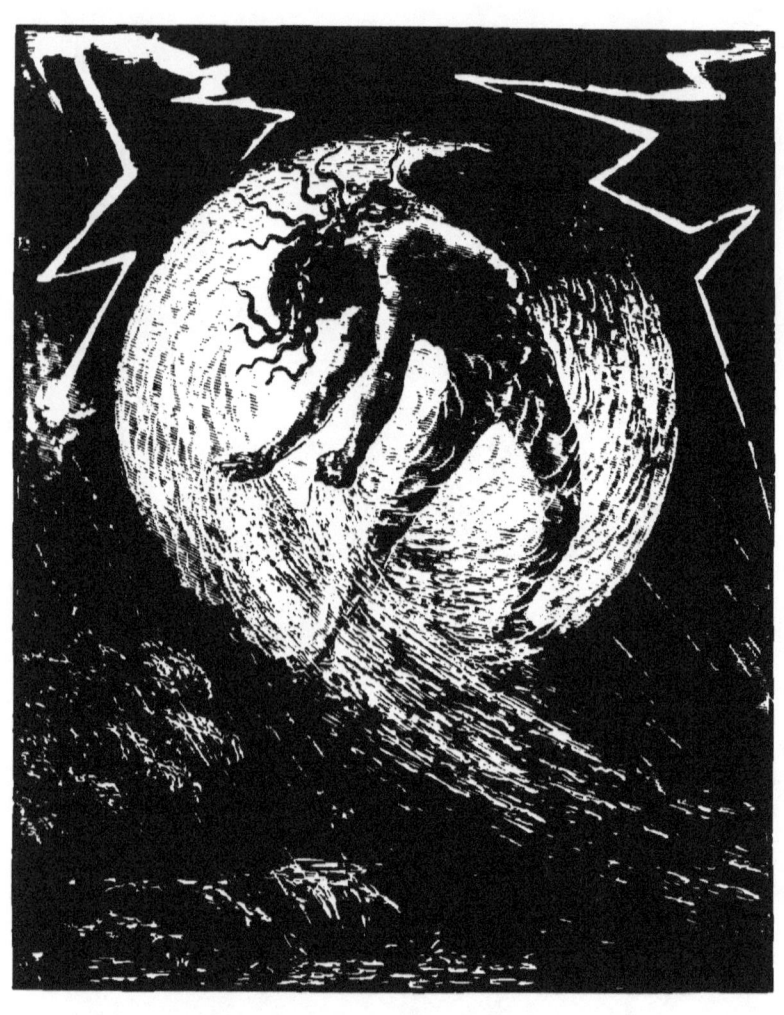

Oh strew, with pausing, shuddering hand,
The seed upon the helpless land,
As if, at every step, ye cast
The pelting hail and riving blast.

IV.

Nay, strew, with free and joyous sweep,
. The seed upon the expecting soil;
For hence the plenteous year shall heap
The garners of the men who toil.

Strew the bright seed for those who tear
The matted sward with spade and share,

And those whose sounding axes gleam
Beside the lonely forest-stream,
.Till its broad banks lie bare ;

And him who breaks the quarry-ledge,
    With hammer-blows, plied quick and strong,

And him who, with the steady sledge,
    Smites the shrill anvil all day long.

Sprinkle the furrow's even trace
  For those whose toiling hands uprear
The roof-trees of our swarming race,
  By grove and plain, by stream and
      mere;

Who forth, from crowded city, lead
    The lengthening street, and overlay
Green orchard-plot and grassy mead
    With pavement of the murmuring way.

Cast, with full hands, the harvest cast,
For the brave men that climb the mast,
When to the billow and the blast
   It swings and stoops, with fearful strain,
And bind the fluttering mainsail fast,
    Till the tossed bark shall sit again,
    Safe as a sea-bird in the main.

V

Fling wide the grain for those who throw
The clanking shuttle to and fro,
In the long row of humming rooms,

And into ponderous masses wind
The web that, from a thousand looms,
Comes forth to clothe mankind.

29

Strew, with free sweep, the grain for them
 By whom the busy thread,
Along the garment's even hem
 And winding seam, is led;
A pallid sisterhood, that keep

 The lonely lamp alight,
In strife with weariness and sleep,
 Beyond the middle night.
Large part be theirs in what the year
Shall ripen for the reaper here.

VI.

Still, strew, with joyous hand, the wheat
On the soft mould beneath our feet,
   For even now I seem
To hear a sound that lightly rings
From murmuring harp and viol's strings,
   As in a summer dream.

The welcome of the wedding
guest,
The bridegroom's look of
bashful pride,
The faint smile of the pallid
bride,

And bridemaid's blush
at matron's jest,
And dance and song
and generous dower
Are in the shining
grains we shower.

VII.

Scatter the wheat for shipwrecked men,
Who, hunger-worn, rejoice again
In the sweet safety of the shore.

And wanderers, lost in woodlands drear,
Whose pulses bound with joy to hear
The herd's light bell once more.

Freely the golden spray be shed
For him whose heart, when night comes down
On the close alleys of the town,
    Is faint for lack of bread.

In chill roof chambers, bleak and bare,
Or the damp cellar's stifling air,
She who now sees, in mute despair,
    Her children pine for food,

Shall feel the dews of gladness start
To lids long tearless, and shall part
The sweet loaf, with a grateful heart,
    Among her thin, pale brood.

Dear, kindly Earth, whose breast we till!
Oh, for thy famished children, fill,
    Where'er the sower walks,
Fill the rich ears that shade the mould
With grain for grain, a hundredfold,
    To bend the sturdy stalks.

VIII.

Strew silently the fruitful seed,
  As softly o'er the tilth ye tread,
For hands that delicately knead
  The consecrated bread.

The mystic loaf that crowns the board,
When, round the table of their Lord,
  Within a thousand temples set,
In memory of the bitter death
Of Him who taught at Nazareth,
  His followers are met,
And thoughtful eyes with tears are wet,
  As of the Holy One they think,
The glory of whose rising, yet
  Makes bright the grave's mysterious brink.

IX.

Brethren, the sower's task is done.
The seed is in its winter bed.
Now let the dark-brown mould be spread,
   To hide it from the sun,
And leave it to the kindly care
Of the still earth and brooding air.

As when the mother, from her breast,
Lays the hushed babe apart to rest,

And shades its eyes and waits to see
How sweet its waking smile will be.

The tempest now may smite, the sleet
All night on the drowned furrow beat,

And winds that, from the cloudy hold,
Of winter breathe the bitter cold,

Stiffen to stone the mellow mould,
Yet safe shall lie the wheat;

Till, out of heaven's unmeasured
    blue,
Shall walk again the genial year,
To wake with warmth and nurse with dew,
The germs we lay to slumber here.

X.

Oh blessed harvest yet to be!
   Abide thou with the love that keeps,
In its warm bosom, tenderly,
   The life which wakes and that which sleeps.

The love that leads the willing spheres
Along the unending track of years,
And watches o'er the sparrow's nest,
Shall brood above thy winter rest,
    And raise thee from the dust, to hold
Light whisperings with the winds of May.

And fill thy spikes
  with living gold,
From summer's
  yellow ray,
Then, as thy garners
  give thee forth,
On what glad errands
  shalt thou go,
Wherever, o'er the
  waiting earth,
Roads wind and
  rivers flow !

The ancient East shall welcome thee
To mighty marts beyond the sea,

And they who dwell where palm-groves sound
To summer winds the whole year round,
Shall watch, in gladness, from the shore,
The sails that bring thy glistening store.

www.ingramcontent.com/pod-product-compliance
Lightning Source LLC
Chambersburg PA
CBHW022203020726
47496CB00008B/2858